Plop was a baby Barn Owl.
He lived with his mummy and daddy
at the top of a tall tree. Plop was the same
as every baby Barn Owl that has ever been –
except for one thing . . .

He was

AFRAID

of the

DARK.

EGMONT

We bring stories to life

First published 1968 by Methuen & Co Ltd
This edition published 2008 by Egmont UK Limited
239 Kensington High Street, London W8 6SA
3 5 7 9 10 8 6 4 2
Text copyright © 1968 The Estate of Jill Tomlinson
Abridgement by permission of the Estate
Illustrations copyright © Paul Howard 2000
Music and songs copyright © Barry Gibson 2008
Recording copyright © Egmont UK Ltd 2008

A CIP catalogue record for this title is available
from the British Library
ISBN 978 1 4052 4075 8
Printed in Singapore

For Philip
and, of course, D.H.
J.T.

For Samuel
P. H.

The Owl Who Was Afraid of the Dark

words by
Jill Tomlinson

illustrated by
Paul Howard

"I don't want to be a night bird," Plop told his mummy. "Dark is nasty."

"You don't know that," she said. "You'd better find out about the dark before you make up your mind. Look, there's a little boy down there. Go and ask him."

So Plop, who was quite new at flying, took a deep breath and flew down.

"Ooh!" cried the little boy as Plop landed with a somersault.

"Hello!" said Plop. "I've come to find out about the dark."

"Oh!" said the boy. "DARK IS EXCITING, especially tonight. We're going to have fireworks!"

"Does it have to be dark?" asked Plop.

"Of course!" replied the boy. "You can't see the fireworks unless it's dark. Look out for them later!"

"Well?" said Mrs Barn Owl when Plop arrived back at the nest.

"The little boy says DARK IS EXCITING," said Plop. "I still do not like it AT ALL! But I will watch the fireworks if you will sit by me."

"We will sit by you," said his mummy and daddy.

So that is what they did.

When the very last firework had faded away, Mr Barn Owl went hunting. All night he brought food back to Plop, until daylight came and it was time for bed.

Halfway through the morning, Plop woke up.

Mrs Barn Owl opened one bleary eye. "Plop, dear," she said, "why don't you find out some more about the dark? Go and ask that old lady in the deck chair."

Plop landed by the old lady with a thump.

"Hello!" he said. "I've come to ask you about the dark. I want to go hunting with Daddy, but he always goes hunting in the dark and I'm afraid of it."

"How very odd," said the lady. "Now, I love the dark. DARK IS KIND. I can forget that I am old and I can sit and remember all the good times."

"I haven't much to remember, yet," said Plop. "I'm rather new, you see."

"Well?" said his mummy, as Plop flew up to the landing branch.

"The old lady says DARK IS KIND," said Plop, "but I still do not like it AT ALL."

That evening, when both his parents went hunting, Plop closed his eyes and tried to remember something to remember. Suddenly he heard a happy shout and Plop forgot about being afraid of the dark. He peered through the leaves and saw a boy sitting by a fire. Plop flew down, landing with an enormous thud.

"Hello!" said Plop. "I've come to see what's going on."

"I'm guarding the camp-fire," said the boy. "The others have gone to play games in the dark, lucky things."

"Do you like the dark?" asked Plop.

"It's super!" the boy replied. "DARK IS FUN. We're going to make cocoa and sing around the fire. Would you like to stay?"

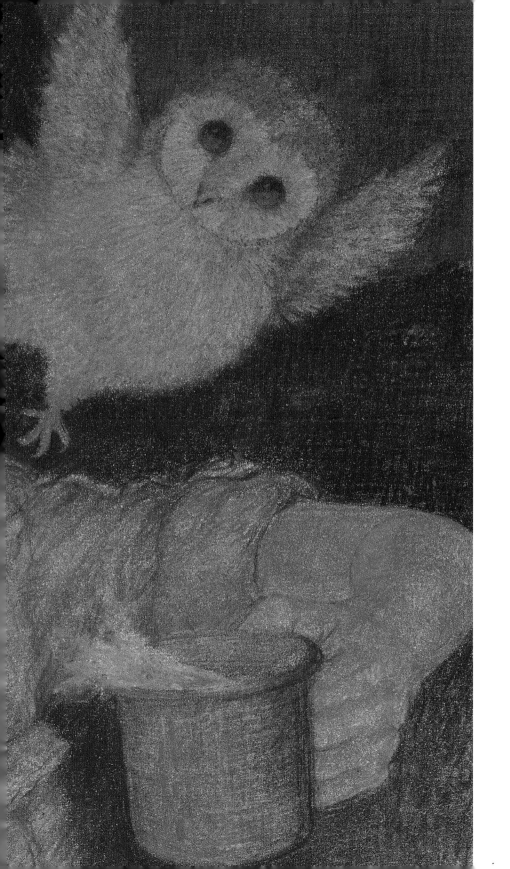

So Plop stayed. The boys sang until the fire had sunk to a red glow. Then Plop said goodbye and flew home.

"Well?" said his mummy. "Where have you been?"

"I met a boy – and he says DARK IS FUN. I still do not like it AT ALL – but I think camp-fires are super!"

Plop woke up the next afternoon and went out on to the landing branch.

"Plop," said Mrs Barn Owl, "go and find out about the dark again. See what that little girl down there thinks about it."

Plop landed by the little girl with a bounce.

"Hello!" he said. "I've come to ask about the dark. Do you like it?"

"Of course I do!" she replied. "DARK IS NECESSARY. Without the dark, Father Christmas wouldn't come. You'd have an empty stocking on Christmas day."

"I don't have a stocking," said Plop. So the little girl took off her wellington and gave him her sock.

"Here," she said, "hang it up on Christmas Eve."

"Oh, thank you!" said Plop and returned to his mummy.

"Well?" said Mrs Barn Owl.

"The little girl says DARK IS NECESSARY, because of Father Christmas coming," Plop said. "I still do not like it AT ALL – but I am going to hang up this sock on Christmas Eve."

Plop slept nearly all day. By evening he was wide awake.

"It's getting-up time, Daddy!" he shouted, butting his father in the tummy.

Mr Barn Owl looked up at the sky. "Not quite yet, Plop," he said. "Wait till it's dark."

That night, Plop watched his parents take off to go hunting again. Looking through the leaves, he saw a man standing on the ground below. So Plop flew down, landing with a gentle bump.

"Heavens!" cried the man. "You startled me."

"Hello!" said Plop. "What's that you've got there?"

"A telescope," said the man. "For looking at the stars and planets at night."

"I don't like the dark very much," said Plop.

"Really?" said the man. "But DARK IS WONDERFUL. I'll show you!"

The man with the telescope showed Plop lots of stars and how they made patterns in the sky. He pointed out the bright Pole Star, the Plough, the Dog Star and Orion the Great Hunter.

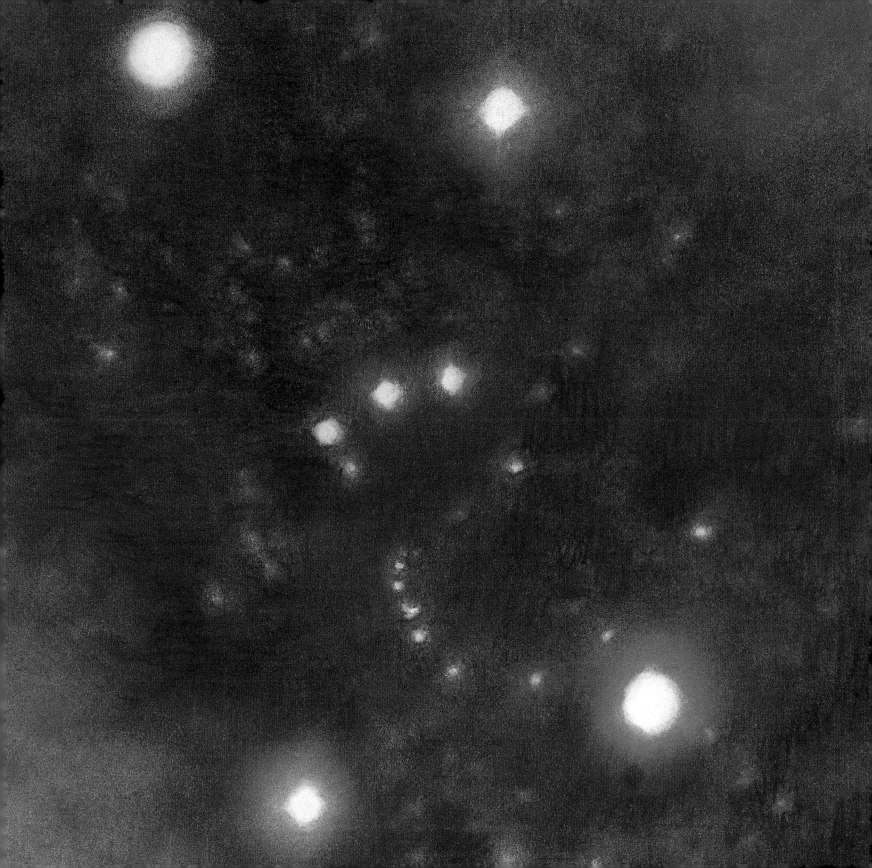

Plop said thank you and flew back to his mummy and daddy.

"A man with a telescope showed me the stars!" Plop told them. "He says DARK IS WONDERFUL!"

That morning Plop had his supper in bed and then, like a real night bird, he slept right through the day.

When Plop woke, it was almost dark. "Now who's a day bird!" he shouted at the darkness. Plop looked at his sleepy parents. He wasn't going to hang about waiting for them. He might be missing something.

Plop floated down and landed like a soft white feather. Under the tree, he saw a big black cat.

"Hello!" said the cat. "I was just going exploring. Won't you come with me?"

"I would like to, I think," said Plop, "but I'm afraid of the dark."

"But DARK IS BEAUTIFUL," said the cat. "Look around you."

Plop looked. The moon had risen. Everything was bathed in its white light.

"Moonlight is magic," said the cat. "Come with me and I will show you the night-time world of cats and owls. Will you come?"

"Yes! I will," said Plop.

The cat took Plop up to the rooftops and they looked down over the sleeping town.

"This is my world!" said Plop. "I am a night bird after all!"

"And this is only one sort of night," said the cat. "There are lots of other kinds, all beautiful."

"Thank you for showing me," said Plop. "I must go now and tell my mummy and daddy."

"Good night," said the black cat, "and many, many Good Nights!"

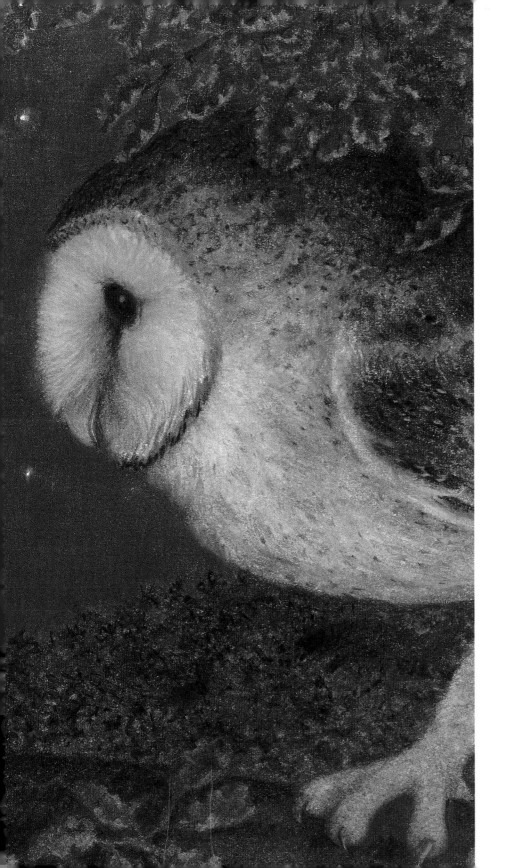

Plop flew straight back to his tree.

"Well?" said his mummy.

Plop took a deep breath.

"The small boy said DARK IS EXCITING. The old lady said DARK IS KIND. The camp-fire boy said DARK IS FUN. The little girl said DARK IS NECESSARY. The man with the telescope said DARK IS WONDERFUL and the black cat said DARK IS BEAUTIFUL."

"And what do you think, Plop?" asked his mummy.

Plop looked up at his parents with twinkling eyes. "I think," he said,

"I think – DARK IS SUPER!"

Then, Plop took off to go hunting
in the dark, Mr and Mrs Barn Owl on
each side and Plop in the middle . . .

Plop –
the night bird.